The Magic of You

A 1Night Stand Story

By
Virginia Cavanaugh

Copyright © 2016 by Virginia Cavanaugh
ISBN: 978-1-68361-040-3
Cover art by Tibbs Designs

Published by
Decadent Publishing Company, LLC

Look for us online at:
www.decadentpublishing.com

~A Note from the Author~

I'm so happy you have decided to take this journey with me. I have a soft spot for magic. I used to play D and D a lot and I tended to lean toward mage characters. For this reason the story The Magic of You was born. I hope you enjoy it.

Best wishes,
Virginia Cavanaugh

authorvirginiacavanaugh@gmail.com
http://www.virginiacavanaugh.com

Dedication

To my husband, Kent. Your unwavering support of my dreams means the world to me.

Chapter One

"Last chance to back out," Susan Kinlow huffed, gripping the steering wheel and trying to work up the courage to exit the car. The idea of backing out didn't appeal. Even though her other run-ins with dating sites had gone badly, she' decided to trust in her friend Kelly's opinion. Hopefully, this time would be different.

Kelly swore by Madame Eve. And Kelly had found extreme happiness with her new husband, Greg. But could Madame Eve really get it right a second time? Kelly seemed to think so. Even went on to say the knack Eve had for pairings bordered on magical. Yeah...like magic existed.

Susan released the wheel and turned her gaze to

the rearview mirror for one last beauty check. Dark locks were arranged in perfect curls on top of her head. A few stray tendrils caressed her neck. She'd gone light on the makeup—the whole less-is-more idea. To hear her mother tell it, she didn't even need it. But, at the ripe old age of thirty, she thought it best to add some coverage. What self-respecting southern girl went anywhere without her face?

A printout of the email Madame Eve sent lay in the passenger seat. A local place had been chosen for their meet up. Stanley's, located on the edge of town, offered a variety of entertainment, including live bands, pool, dancing, darts, and drinks.

She looked at the front door of the establishment. "Here goes nothing."

She grabbed her small purse and exited the car. The click-clack of her heels echoed against the asphalt parking lot. Anticipation and nervousness coursed through her body. Deep down she feared how he'd look at the inner book nerd side of her who loved fantasy. Most guys didn't find it sexy. The few guys she'd met who did see it as a turn-on, she'd either not been attracted to or they'd come with a side of crazy. But she'd answered the questionnaire honestly, and if Kelly hadn't exaggerated, then she should find a man inside with similar tastes. She barely repressed the need to roll her eyes. Did such a man even exist?

A tall male stood at the entrance. Tanned skin stretched tight over large biceps. His dark eyes gleamed in the low light. He looked every part the bouncer he was. Surely, knowing this man would be the one to settle the issues, most patrons would think twice before starting any crap. He checked Susan's ID and then opened the door, allowing her to enter.

Striding into the club, she nodded her head slightly to the beat of the streaming smooth jazz music. She took a second to adjust to the low glow provided by sleek stylish wall sconces. It offered a candlelit quality, providing a great atmosphere for seduction. In the right corner, band members stood on a stage. Small round tables lined the sides of a dance floor. Against the back wall, two bartenders mixed drinks at whirlwind speed. Plenty of people milled around the place, but at least it wasn't overcrowded. The low hum of conversation blended into the mix of noise.

Susan searched through the sea of people, looking for her date. Jason Hendrick. The email said he was tall, blond, and would be wearing a red button-down shirt with a black tie. To help him identify her, she also wore red. The strapless dress accented her large breasts and flared from the waistline, skimming her knees.

The longer she looked without spotting him, the more nervous she became. Her heart rate accelerated. Had he stood her up? God, she hoped not. It was hard to get back into the dating ring. Being stood up would be a huge slap to her confidence.

"Susan?"

The deep male voice resounded from behind her, and she jumped, turning in his direction. Swallowing hard, she stared at the handsome man, his blond hair styled in a devil-may-care way. *Holy hotness*! Even in the low light, his bright-blue eyes shone. The corners of his sexy full mouth tipped upward to show off a small dimple in his left cheek.

"I'm sorry. I didn't mean to startle you."

Susan blinked to clear her thoughts and found

her voice. "It's fine." She looked down and noticed the red shirt and black tie. The material did little to disguise his defined pectoral muscles. Her gaze rose back to his. "You must be Jason?"

Straight white teeth were revealed with his smile. "Yes. It's nice to meet you, Susan."

She accepted his offered hand, gave it a quick shake then released it. The heat from his palm warmed her and made her pulse increase. Must be her nervousness. After all, it had only been a handshake.

"Sorry I'm a little late. This is the first time I've been here," Jason said.

"Not a problem. I just arrived myself."

"How about we find a table and order a couple of drinks?"

She nodded and allowed him to guide her across the room. The warm calloused skin against hers made her more aware of him as a man. Nope. It wasn't just nerves. Something in his touch had her body tingling. From her vantage point slightly behind him, she couldn't resist the urge to analyze his ass, an asset of perfection framed in black dress slacks. A warning formed in her brain. Could this guy be too good to be true?

"Is this spot all right with you?" he asked, pulling out a chair for her.

"Yeah." She sat down. There were four seats to choose from, yet he took the one to her left then signaled a waitress.

"I don't mean to be forward, but I have to let you know you look absolutely stunning," he said.

She focused on his face, a warm flush of appreciation swimming through her veins. A small laugh escaped her lips, nervousness still riding her hard. "Thanks. You look nice, too."

Truth be told, downright sexy would be a better description.

The waitress approached them and took their drink orders. Jason hardly spared a look in her direction. Susan thought it slightly odd since the other woman was definitely attractive and showing ample amounts of cleavage. Most men she knew would at least give the waitress a second glance. Maybe even a flirty smile. But Jason continued to stare in her direction, and she kind of liked knowing she held his attention. "So, you said you've never been here before."

"Yeah. I live nearly a couple hours from here in Lubbock. I don't come this way often."

Interesting. She'd been to Lubbock. People from this area used their medical facilities often. "You've never even come here to visit the casino?" The casino was a new addition to Lea County and tended to bring people in flocks to gamble or watch the horse races.

"Sadly, no. Free time can be hard to come by in my line of work."

Amen to that. Work tied her up quite a bit. Meetings over future building projects kept her close to home. "There's something we have in common, then. I work for a local construction company. With the way Hobbs is growing, getting time off can be very hard. What do you do?"

"I'm in sales. Have you lived in this area all of your life?"

"Yes. Born and raised here." She sipped her wine, wondering why he didn't elaborate on his field of work. "W-what type of sales are you in?"

His brow twitched. "I run a shop dealing in a multitude of different things. Books, candles...novelty stuff."

"Sounds interesting." Not exactly what she'd imagined him saying. When he said sales, she thought more along the lines of something in the oil field, seeing how that particular industry boomed in this area, at least for the time being. The older population tended to always warn another oil crash could be right around the corner.

"It has its moments." He took a drink of his whiskey and soda. "Enough about work. What do you like to do for fun?"

She inhaled a deep breath. Time to put it on the table. "I'm actually kind of boring."

Jason arched a brow. "I don't believe you."

"Really? What if I told you I like to curl up on the couch and watch movies, or read a book?"

A seductive grin spread across his lips, and he leaned a little closer. "I'd say watching a movie with someone can be fun. Especially if said someone is as beautiful as you are." He leaned back. "And reading is a good pastime."

Her blood heated at the thought of snuggling with him under a blanket. Would he skim his hand along her leg and squeeze her thigh, or would he be more subtle in his touches? Maybe a mock stretch, bringing his arm around her shoulders?

"What movies do you like to watch, Susan?"

Her name on his lips was like a caress against her skin. She shivered with awareness and wiggled in her seat slightly. "I like all types."

He moved toward her, his warm breath gliding along the sensitive skin of her neck. "But what is your favorite?"

Her lids lowered to half-mast, and she contemplated an answer. Would he think her a big nerd if she answered truthfully? Trying to think or care at all had become hard with him inching closer. Should she be freaked out? Things were moving a little fast. But she liked him close. A strange sense of awareness flooded her veins. Yes, she definitely liked him close. Attraction sizzled between them. Sensual nerve impulses danced across her skin, causing a tingling sensation. What had he even asked?

"Drama? Comedy? Maybe even horror?"

Yes. That was it. He wanted to know her favorite type of movie. "To be honest, I like movies with a medieval theme."

"Ah. She wants to be the princess who's rescued from the tower."

More of a statement than a question. Did she want to be rescued? She gazed into his eyes. A little less than a foot separated them. If he was doing the rescuing? She sat up straighter and reached for her wine. "I don't know. Maybe." She took a drink and tried to get her pulse under control. "What about you? What sort of movie interests you?"

"Actually, I like medieval-themed movies, too. And I'm not just saying that to make it sound like we have a connection. I'd have to say one of my all-time favorites is *Willow*."

She couldn't contain her excitement. "Really? I love *Willow*."

He laughed. "Is it so hard to believe? It's not like I named some chick flick."

She giggled. "True. Most guys are into the shoot-em-up type Rambo movies. Does this make you a closet nerd?"

"Who said anything about a closet? I'm a full-out nerd."

His sexy-as-sin mouth delivered a grin, making her insides buzz with want. "Full-out nerd, eh? Like I play Dungeons & Dragons full-out nerd, or I just watch the Syfy Channel on occasion?" If he said D&D, she'd really have to evaluate if this was too good to be true.

"I used to DM."

"No way." *Him. A dungeon master. What type of adventures would he come up with?* The possibilities were endless. Visions of role playing with him turned into real-life fantasies, ending with their limbs entwined, both finding their happy ending.

Jason took a slow drink. "Yep. I'm guessing you play, too?"

Skin flushed from her musings, she had to shake off the desire riding her to pay attention. "Not since high school, but yeah. I love the game. You don't find a lot of people playing it any more. Or more should I say it's hard to find a good dungeon master."

She sat back in her chair and stared. Calling him Master would be an immense turn-on. Where had that thought come from? She wasn't usually the kinky sort. It had to be his comment on rescuing her from a tower earlier. Seriously, what were the chances she'd meet a hot guy who liked the nerdy stuff she did? Maybe Madame Eve had a little magic in her after all.

"What type of character did you play?" Jason took a slow drink.

He swallowed, the muscles in his throat working. Funny how a man taking a drink could be erotic. She took a sip of her own, trying to clear her mind before she answered. "Kyanna is an elf paladin. I created her in my teens. I haven't played the game in about seven years."

"Truth be told, I haven't played for years either."

"What was the name of the character you created?" She really wanted to know more about this man, who seemed to have the power to turn her on in both mind and body.

"Finlock. A human mage."

"For some reason, I pictured you to be more of the ranger type." She took a sip of her wine. Maybe even a thief who'd scale a castle wall, sneaking into her bedchamber to rob her of her virtue. The thought nearly made her snort. It had been a while since she had "virtue" to steal, so to speak. But this was a fantasy, so who gave a damn if she invented a new virtue?

The corners of his mouth lifted in mirth. "I've always had a thing for magic."

She looked down at the table and grinned. Suddenly, the fantasy took a different shape. He had enchanted her. Magic. It somehow fit better. This calm, seductive spell he seemed to cast on her canceled out her fears to leave a sexually charged calm.

"What?"

Susan redirected her gaze to his handsome face. "I was really nervous about tonight. I mean, I'm kind of a nerd. I guess what I'm trying to say is, I feel a little more comfortable."

"Good. Because I really like you. I know we just met, but I want to get to know you. And it would be easier to do if you feel comfortable."

Wow. She couldn't believe how well things were going. In the back of her mind, she waited for the other shoe to drop. This guy couldn't be this perfect.

He had to be hiding something. The evasion of work-related questions was kind of a red flag. What could he be hiding there? "Tell me a little more about the shop you run."

"I'd rather know more about what you like."

She traced her index finger around the rim of her glass. "Is there something bad about your work?" *Here we go.* She concentrated on the wine, waiting for him to answer.

"No. I just don't think our jobs should define us. There's so much more that goes into making us who we are. For instance, I also like Comic-Con."

Her gaze snapped to his. "You've gone to Comic-Con?"

"Yeah. I got to go the year James Cameron talked about *Avatar*. I don't get a lot of free time, but I tend to use what I do get wisely. I had a good time."

Part of her knew he dodged her on the work question, but she'd let it slide for the time being. It could be he didn't make a lot of money and it embarrassed him. But she wasn't shallow enough to worry about such trivial things. Of course, he'd have to get to know her better before he realized it. "I'd really like to go sometime. Maybe work will slow down in the near future and I can get a chance, too."

"Maybe, sometime, we can go together."

Heat washed through her veins at the thought of spending time with him. Would they share a room? Thoughts of his hands on her skin invaded her mind. Why had her musing returned to this? Probably because she knew, before the night ended, she would be crawling into bed with him. The thought excited her. Someone could always back out of the deal of sleeping together. She hoped he wouldn't. For some reason, she had a feeling he would be awesome in bed. But going out of town with him? Why would she even consider it when they'd only met an hour ago? Because she liked him, and, even if the other shoe dropped, she wanted to stick around and see how it went. "Maybe."

The band in the corner started playing a slower song. Jason glanced at them and then returned his gaze to her eyes. "Would you dance with me?"

Dancing had never really been her strong suit, but since a slow song played she figured swaying to the beat should be easy enough. She nodded and accepted his hand.

He turned her to face him, tightening his grip slightly. She didn't resist when he pulled her near, settling his opposite hand on her hip. Her fingers slid up his arm, feeling the powerful muscles before coming to rest on his shoulder. Regular workouts must be a part of his life because no way did he get built like this by running a store.

Heat spread across her skin, radiating from every area he touched. A swirl of desire moved through her body, causing her to tingle in anticipation. She didn't remember ever being this attracted to a man before.

"This is a nice place. I'm glad you chose it."

Her gaze met his. "I like jazz and most places here play country."

"Do you have something against country?" A teasing grin spread across his lips. "I'm from Texas after all."

She laughed. "No. It's all right on occasion."

"I listen to all types of music. But this is nice."

She matched his steady sway, noticing during each small step their bodies drifted closer. Her breasts grazed his chest, the slight movement teasing her nipples beneath her dress. They hardened in response, and she had to repress the sigh wanting to escape her lips.

His hand moved from her hip to the small of her back, pressing her more firmly to him. "I like being close to you."

Her cheek brushed his. Only slight stubble peppered the side of his face. Enough to arouse but not abrade. "I like it, too." What harm would there be in admitting it? He had. And, right now, she definitely enjoyed feeling his firm body against her.

"I'm really trying not to sound like a creep. I sure as hell don't want to scare you away."

She smiled. "If it helps, you aren't giving me the *Chester the Molester* vibe."

He laughed. "Well, that's good to know."

She hesitated to tell him she felt it, too. A sense of rightness about being here with him filled her. Could there really be such a thing as soul mates? She resisted rolling her eyes at the thought. A difference existed between living in a fantasy land and being a fan of fantasy. It would be safer to stick to being a fan, but her earlier musings surfaced in her mind.

Would it be so bad to live in the fantasy for one night?

"Are you having a good time?"

She turned her face toward his shoulder, inhaling his scent, the warm feeling of arousal and happiness tipping the corners of her mouth up. The aroma was moan worthy. Spice and maybe a hint of musk. Not trusting herself to speak, she nodded.

"Me, too."

For the next few moments, she laid her head on his chest and relaxed against him, listening to his heart beat strong and steady. They swayed to the sensual music, and his chin came to rest on top of her head. Their bodies seemed to fit nicely against each other.

Arousal, desire, caution, and insecurity waged a war inside her. Her attraction to Jason was off the charts. Never before had she slept with a man on the first date, but she found herself excited about Jason being her first. She'd never expected a ring or anything in the past, but usually the clothes didn't come off unless she'd been with a guy for a while. But the way her body blazed made her yearn to feel his skin against hers. She pressed her chest closer to his, tilted her head and met his stare.

His gaze fell to her lips. Would he kiss her?

She inhaled deeply, bringing their upper bodies even closer. She wanted him to kiss her—the thought both shocking and thrilling her. Muscled hardness molded to her softer curves. The powerful hand on her lower back moved to her opposite hip, encircling her in his embrace. She wanted to know what his kiss would feel like—what his lips would taste like. Things were moving fast, but she didn't want to put the brakes on. The warning siren in her brain screaming caution went ignored. She wanted this adventure, and, for once, she was going to step up and take it.

Easing to her tiptoes, she closed the distance between them. Their mouths met—a tantalizing graze of skin against skin. Testing. Tempting. The electric shock of it teased her nerves, making her want more.

He let go of her hand and cupped the side of her face, taking control of the kiss.

A moan of pleasure broke free of her, and she parted her lips, welcoming his tongue into her mouth. The sensual glide and pull of his lips shot desire to new heights. His taste inebriated her. A smooth hint of his whiskey and soda blended with pure passion.

Their lips parted, and she sucked in a breath. Slightly dazed, she blinked and tried to focus on his eyes.

"I'm sorry," he whispered.

Chapter Two

*S*orry? She shook her head, trying to clear the passion fog enveloping her brain. "I don't understand." Did he think her a lousy kisser or something?

Jason's palm fell from her face, reclaimed her hand then led her off of the dance floor toward a dimly lighted hallway. Confused, she followed him, but slowed her steps when she saw the sign for the restrooms. If he thought she would be down for a quick romp in a public bathroom, he was out of his mind. Besides, she hated to even use a public restroom. The idea of doing anything else in there turned her off. Yet, he'd said sorry. She retracted her fingers from his, wanting to know what in the hell was going on.

He cast an apologetic look. "I didn't mean for things to go so far so fast."

Oh hell. This better not be where he tells me he's married. Maybe she should've been a little more concerned with the other shoe dropping. She put her hands up in a no-harm-no-foul gesture. "You don't have to explain. I'll just go." Damn it if this hadn't turned out bad like the other setups. She turned to leave, but he grabbed her arm gently.

"Susan, wait...."

She spun halfway around. "Why? Either you're married or you weren't into the kiss. I don't need to know. It's fine." She just wanted to get the hell out of here. Heat filled her face. Embarrassment sucked. Disappointment hurt.

He pulled her into his arms, the gentleness gone, replaced with a power that didn't threaten but spoke of dominance. Her back met the wall, and he pressed his body close.

"I'm not married, and I was damn well into every second of our kiss."

Her core throbbed and pulsed at his words.

"I only meant I didn't mean for things to

progress fast. I don't want you to feel rushed." He pressed his pelvis against her lower belly. "You can tell, I wasn't unaffected by a long shot.

The length of his erection impressed her. She sighed, her nether lips growing wet with wanting him.

"But this isn't the right place. And, as much as the honorable side of me wants to return to the table and finish our date, the side of me wanting to strip you bare and kiss every inch of you is winning. The taste of your kiss still burns on my tongue. Sin and sexual promise. It makes me want to know what the rest of your sexy body tastes like."

She repressed a moan. No man had ever spoken so boldly to her. She should probably be freaked out, but she liked it.

"But I don't want you to do anything you might regret, and I sure as hell don't want to mess things up with you. I like you, Susan."

"I like you, too."

"I'm going to write down the name of the hotel I'm staying at and the room number. Take some time to decide if you want to meet me there. I know we went into this meet up with the knowledge of where it would end up, but I don't want you to feel obligated. If you want to sleep with me, I want you to do it because you want to. And no matter what your decision is, I'll be calling you tomorrow."

Susan couldn't stop the smile spreading across her face. He led them to the bar and borrowed a pen and paper from the bartender. Jason scribbled down the information then folded it into a square. He pulled her close, kissing her on the cheek and pressing the piece of paper into her hand.

"I hope you come to me," he whispered. He released her hand and walked away, exiting the club. She trembled in his wake.

Holy shit! Her body burned with desire. She followed him. Obligation had nothing to do with the need coursing through her. Outside, the cool night air danced across her skin, the door swinging shut behind her. She tried to locate Jason, but he was nowhere to be found. His speed in leaving only served to heighten her excitement.

Her heels *click-clacked* loudly as she half jogged to her car. Once inside, she released a giggle, taking a long, hard look at herself in the rearview mirror. Her skin flushed, but her makeup and hair remained in order. The sight of her kiss-swollen lips heightened her anticipation.

Fingers trembling, she unfolded the paper and read the address.

She pressed the start button. The engine revved to life, and she backed out of the parking lot. Resisting the urge to speed across town proved hard—especially since she seemed to catch every stoplight. Doubt crept up her spine and she shivered. *What am I thinking? I shouldn't meet him at his hotel.*

No. I want to get laid, damn it. She tried hard to push those pestering thoughts aside. *But what if?*

She released a groan, willing the light to change faster. *What if this remains a one-night stand? He said he'd call regardless, but what do I really know about him? Maybe I should just go home and wait for his call tomorrow. But what if he doesn't?*

She ground her teeth. This could be her one chance to have hot sex with Jason. Missing out on this opportunity wasn't an option. So what if she'd never had a one-night stand before? There's always a first time for everything. And if she slept with him and he didn't call, she'd eventually get over it. Wouldn't she? She ground her teeth in frustration. Who ever won anything without taking risks? And the prize of a mind-blowing night of hot sex she definitely wanted to win.

The light turned green, and she remained on her path. It should only take another fifteen minutes to reach his hotel. Fifteen minutes to fight her doubts and cram them into a tiny corner of her mind.

When she caught the next red light, she wanted to yell. Was the universe trying to tell her something? She laughed. "That would be like believing in magic, which is silly."

She sucked in a fortifying breath. It was just sex. And these were just traffic lights. "I seriously need to chill."

The sign for his hotel sat ahead on the right. She pulled into the parking lot, squirming in her seat. Luckily, she found a space close to the front. *Showtime.* Brushing off the rest of her nervousness, she exited the car and headed for the main entrance.

Susan glanced at the paper. His handwriting looked masculine in the extreme. No bubbly loops in the harsh slanting lines. Room number 123. On the first floor.

She ambled through the lobby, casting a shy grin to the clerk on duty, but didn't pause. She really didn't want to speak to him because she knew her face would flush. And surely he'd know what she was about to do. Lucky for her, he didn't ask. *Sometimes it pays to look like you know where you're going.*

A sign ahead showed Jason's room number to be to her left. She moved closer to her destination, lust flaring low in her belly. The sway of her dress against her legs stimulated her like a tempting caress. Madness. Exhilarating madness. The door marked with his number came into view. Her nipples hardened. She raised her fist to knock, willing her hand to stop trembling.

The door swung open.

She stared at Jason, and her breath caught. The black tie was gone, and the buttons of his shirt had been freed. Sculpted muscles lay revealed within the opening, along with a slight dusting of blond hair on his chest and belly.

"You came."

His softly spoken words brought her gaze to his. The desire zinging between them couldn't be denied. He stepped back, and she entered the room. Gaze lowering to the tightly woven blue-and-gray carpet, she noticed his bare feet.

He stepped past her. The soft click of the door closing and the tap of metal sounded behind her. The locks had been engaged, preventing anyone from entering even if they had a key.

"I'm glad you're here, Susan." He stood behind her and traced his hands down her arms.

She leaned back. The skin of her shoulder blades met the warm skin of his chest. Warmth from his body consumed her like a blanket. She sighed, lowering her eyelids as his hands snaked around her waist. He molded her to his body—his hard cock pressed against her bottom. Wetness spread across her nether lips.

He kissed her neck. "I don't know how I got this lucky," he breathed into her ear.

She tilted her head to the side, wanting more of

his mouth on her skin. "What do you mean?"

"To have a beautiful, smart woman like you in my arms."

"We're both lucky." She faced him then took slow, retreating steps.

He stalked her until her back met a cool wall. She shivered. It took only a moment before he caged her, his palms on the wall on both sides of her head, and his hot body pressed against her.

When their lips met, an explosion of arousal danced through her blood. No gentleness could be found in the kiss. He devoured her mouth. His ravenous hunger matched hers. Tongues danced with sensual glides, carrying her deeper into the pool of pleasure.

She glided her hands inside his shirt, wanting to feel his strength. The muscles rippled beneath her palms, and he pressed even closer, sliding his hands over her hips to grip her ass. He ground his pelvis against hers, and a wonderful sensation filled her pussy, making her throb. The need to feel him inside her grew. But there were way too many clothes between them.

Urgency clawed inside her, and she pushed at his shirt. He relinquished his hold on her long enough to let it fall down his arms and to the floor then he went for the zipper at the back of her dress. The material parted, and she shimmied, allowing it to slip free and pool around her feet. His fingers worked the clasp of her strapless bra, and he stepped back, letting it tumble to the floor.

The half-growl half-moan he released made her squirm, desire riding her hard. She bowed her back, thrusting her achy breasts out and squeezing her thighs together to try and calm the pulsing in her pussy.

"So fucking sexy." He leaned in and captured one pert nipple in his mouth.

Warm. Wet. His lips teased and tempted her flesh. She gasped, holding his head in place. The graze of his teeth against the taut bud had her crying out in pleasure and pain—a wonderful mix of sensations. He pinched one nipple while he nibbled the other peak. Intense passion had her clawing at his shoulders and panting with need.

"Please," she whispered and moved against the

wall. She needed more. Orgasm hovered just beyond reach, taunting her with wicked promise.

Releasing her breasts, his hands returned to her lace-covered ass, lifting her. She wrapped her arms around his neck and her legs around his hips. Mouths melded once more in a searing kiss.

He grazed his teeth across her lower lip as he broke contact to toss her on the bed. She bounced a little, and her gaze landed on him, moving from head to toe. The intense look on his face enhanced his attraction. Powerful, broad shoulders led to well-defined pecs, tapering to a trim waist and cut abs. His dress pants rode low on his hips, revealing the waistband of his boxers. The head of his hard cock peeked out of the band. She licked her lips, wanting to taste him. The sexy growl-moan combo rumbled in his throat, causing her to tingle in anticipation.

His gaze moved over her body like a caress. Normally, her nervousness about showing off her curves dimmed her desire, but Jason seemed to enjoy her thicker areas. In fact, his hungry expression made her feel like the sexiest woman in the world.

He gripped her left ankle and met her gaze—

working loose the strap on her heel. The shoe slipped free, hitting the floor. He massaged her arch with gentle strokes. Then he repeated the deed on the other side.

When he released her other foot and stripped off his pants and boxers, she bit her bottom lip. His turgid cock sprang free, and her tongue glided across the opening over her mouth. Not too big and not too small.

Susan spread her knees, welcoming the weight of his body. He licked and nipped at her mouth before claiming it in a searing kiss. The glide and pull turned into a soft, sensual flow of tongues tangling. She couldn't get enough of his taste. Whiskey and man.

His mouth slid to her neck, delivering hot kisses and teeth grazing her flesh. Goose bumps erupted down her arms and back. She inhaled his scent. Spice and clean sweat. His lips trailed lower, across the valley of her breasts, stopping to kiss and tongue her navel before proceeding farther. She realized his intent, and her inner muscles clenched tight in anticipation. It had been a while since a guy went down on her.

"I need to taste you." He gripped the sides of her lace panties and pulled them down her legs, briefly rising to his feet to pull them free of her body and toss them on the floor.

The tip of his tongue traced the seam of her pussy. A staggered breath filled her lungs, and she released it on a moan. He used his thumbs to spread her open and set to kissing her there with slow, sensual wickedness.

"Feels good." She speared her hands into his hair and lifted her hips. The growl he released rumbled against her needy flesh.

Sounds of pleasure burst through her lips as he continued to tease her with his tongue. He sucked her clit, and the familiar fullness and throbbing of her inner muscles signaled her approaching orgasm. She gave in and let the sensual tide crest. Jason moaned, strengthening to force of her release.

Her muscles trembled and Jason climbed over her body. He kissed her soundly and reached toward the nightstand. The essence of her passion on his lips drove her arousal to new heights. She wanted him inside her.

He released her mouth and tore open the small foil packet with his teeth. Reaching between their bodies, he rolled the condom over his cock. The head of his erection traced her labia, parting the slick flesh before pushing deep inside. A gasp tore from her lips, and she wiggled her hips to try to adjust to the fullness of his erection. It had been a while since she'd taken a lover. She undulated beneath him, shifting him deeper.

"You're so tight," he moaned then pulled out and pushed back in again. Ripples of pleasure danced through her pussy.

"Please," she cried, needing him to move.

He started a slow pace. Each time he pressed his pelvis hard against hers, applying pressure to her clit. He kissed her, matching the sensual motion of his cock with his tongue. It drove her mad. She writhed beneath him.

His lips tore away from hers on a laugh. "Impatient are we?" He reached down and hooked her knee into the crook of his elbow, bringing her leg up, fucking her deeper.

"Yes!" she cried out, bowing her back.

His hips pumped against her, increasing his pace. The satisfying smack of skin against skin filled the air, mixing with the sounds of their pleasure. She dug her nails into his shoulders and held on tight as her climax erupted. The pulsing in her pussy milked him, begging for his release. With a shout, he gave in. The throbbing of his cock provoked a new round of spasms. She sighed, her body trembling in the aftermath of one of the best climaxes she'd ever had.

Jason released her leg and lowered his upper body against hers, sweat-slickened skin touching hers. He claimed her lips in a slow, satisfying kiss.

After a few seconds, he rolled away from her and lay on his back. She flipped onto her side and tucked her hands beneath her cheek.

He smiled. "Wow."

"I agree." A satisfied grin pulling at the corners of her mouth.

Jason looked down his body. "Give me a minute. I need to go dispose of this." He scooted off the bed, and she giggled. He peered over his shoulder, making his way to the bathroom. "Don't move one sexy inch of your body."

She blushed, checking out his nude form. Firm muscles everywhere. "What if I'm not comfortable?" she teased.

"Okay. Just don't leave the bed." He disappeared from her view.

Gooseflesh rose all over her skin, and she shivered. The absence of his body heat had her crawling under the covers. Would she stay the rest of the night? Did he even want her to?

She frowned and rolled onto her side, her back facing the bathroom door. When she glanced toward the window, a weird reddish glow emanated from behind the curtain. She bolted up in the bed, clutching the covers to her chest. "What in the hell is that?"

It damn well better not be a recording device.

Chapter Three

"Shit!" Jason darted to the end of the bed and stabbed his legs into his pants.

"Did you just record what we did?"

His gaze pinned her. "What? No! It's complicated." He bent and retrieved her dress from the floor and tossed it to her. "I can explain, but, for your safety, I need you to get dressed fast."

She stared at him—eyes wide, jaw slack. Dammit. He didn't want her to find out like this. "Please. We have to go. Now."

Susan tossed the covers off, exited the bed, and marched to the window where she pulled the curtain aside. "It's a rock." She picked up the glowing stone and turned around, confusion furrowing her brow.

"Not just a rock. It's a crystal."

"What in the hell is going on?"

Jason bent to pick up Susan's discarded underclothes. This date had been doomed from the get-go. "It's not like you're going to believe me if I tell you."

"Try me."

They needed to get away from here. Maybe the truth would make her dress faster, if only to get away from him. "I'm not in sales. I made it up. I'm a warlock. And when the stone glows red, it means something ugly is nearby and I need to get you away from it."

She dropped the stone. "Oh dear God. You're crazy." She pulled her clothes on. "I knew something wasn't right. This was too good to be true."

At least she had started to dress, even if she did think him nuts. "I'm telling you the truth, no matter how hard it is to believe." He should have turned down the job last night, but the head of his coven put him on a guilt trip. Of course, it hadn't been until after he'd dispatched the Hilex Demon running loose in Odessa that his leader informed him the SOB had a brother. No doubt the fucker had come to seek revenge on him.

Susan sat on the end of the bed and slipped on her heels. "I can't believe this. Magic isn't real."

"It's very real."

"Then prove it." She crossed her arms over her chest.

He glanced at the stone on the floor, and it changed from red to black. "Looks like I might have to." Without any further explanation, he grabbed her arm and dragged her to the door.

"What do you think you're doing?" She tried to yank free.

He whispered a quick incantation to open her eyes to his world. "We have company."

The window behind them shattered, and Susan screamed. Jason didn't take any time to look behind them, knowing full well what she saw. The Helix Demons were pretty large and scary bull-like creatures. Blood-red snot and drool no doubt leaked down his ugly mug. If he could have chosen something else for her to see in his strange world, he would've. But there wasn't any way to ease her into his paranormal realm. And chances were better than good she'd never want to see him again after this. He flung the door wide and pulled her along behind him to the exit at the end of the hallway.

A fireball flew in front of them as an angry growl emanated from behind. Fire blocked their path. Alarms blared. Jason took the stairs. Good news? Susan had gotten with the program, and he no longer had to pull her along.

"Holy shit! What is that thing?"

He grabbed her arm and pulled her in front of him on the staircase, his other hand on her back urging her up the stairs.

She stomped up the remaining stairs. Someone had to be playing a prank on her. Then again, the fire sure seemed real. People flooded the hallways, in various states of dress, the detectors in the ceiling wailing an ear-splitting alarm. Jason yelled, ordering people to go the other way to keep them from running into the fire at the bottom of the stairwell.

Susan followed the crowd, hoping they could

make it to the other set of stairs. A powerful hand encircled her arm, and she yelped, stumbling as Jason pulled her into a vacant room. "What the hell? I thought we were getting out of here!"

He released her arm and strode to the window. "The demon will be waiting for us down there."

"What about all those other people? If it's true, they're running to their deaths." She rushed to his side. "We have to tell them."

He gripped her upper arms. "Those other people are fine. They won't even notice the demon downstairs."

"How in the hell are they not going to notice a big red-and-black bull-looking dude with sharp teeth and a bleeding nose?"

He grimaced. "Because the only reason you saw his true form is because I cast a spell on you to open your eyes."

She shook her head. Had she really just asked about a scary creature downstairs? *This has to be a dream. This stuff isn't real.* "This is a prank, isn't it?"

Jason sighed. "I wish it were, but no. This is real. This is why I didn't go into detail about my job."

She allowed him to pull her into his embrace. She trembled. Part of her held out for this to all be a dream. Surely, she'd fallen asleep on the bed while Jason was in the bathroom. *Or maybe he spiked my drink with LSD.* She took solace in his warmth. *But this feels real.* She felt his hard, muscular body against hers. The heat from those flames had felt real, too.

She pulled back and stared up at his face. He looked down at her, his brow creased with concern and sadness. "This is real, isn't it?"

"I'm sorry, Susan."

"Holy shit this is real." She glanced at the closed door.

"We can't get out that way." He tucked his finger beneath her chin, drawing her attention. "I need you to trust me."

"Okay, but how do you plan to get us out of here?"

His gaze went to the window, and Susan had to swallow past a lump in her throat. Fear could be crippling, and she couldn't afford to give it any more power. She sucked in a fortifying breath. "All right.

What do we need to do?"

He pulled her body against his and whispered words in a language she didn't understand. The window shattered, glass falling in a rain of tinkling noise to the pavement below.

"Please tell me we don't have to jump."

He frowned. "I'd be lying."

"Fine." Closing her eyes, she tried to regain control of her nerves. "At least tell me we won't die when we hit the ground."

"That I can promise you."

He stepped up on the sill and held her hand, assisting her up next to him. *Damn. That's a long way down.* White rocks lined the flower bed, along with various greenery which didn't look like it would be too helpful in breaking their fall.

"Trust me," he whispered, and squeezed her hand.

She nodded, not daring to speak. Somehow, she held the scream inside when they leapt. Her dress whipped at her legs. She closed her eyes, refusing to watch the pavement speeding closer. Jason gave a command, syllables and foreign sound filling the air around her, and their descent slowed right before their feet touched the ground.

A laugh escaped her lips, and she looked up at his face. Yeah, it sounded like a mix of hysteria and relief, but what the hell? Magic was real.

"Let's go." Jason tugged her hand, and they bolted into the pasture behind the hotel.

"Where are we going?" Running in heels was so cliché, but it beat the alternative of getting a foot full of stickers or mesquite thorns.

"My SUV is parked out this way."

Her head whipped to the side. "Did you expect this?" She stumbled, and he steadied her then swung her up in his arms and moved even faster.

"Well, I had hoped it wouldn't happen, but I couldn't exclude the possibility."

She didn't know what to think. She'd been worried about him thinking her a nerd while he'd been worrying about possible demon attacks. The whole thing blew her mind.

Behind some taller mesquite bushes sat a Jeep. The white glow of the moon bathed the area in a soft light. Jason released his hold and allowed her feet to touch the ground.

In a rush, they both climbed inside, and he started the engine. She pushed her hair out of her face and took in a few deep breaths, hoping to slow her heart rate. "So, where exactly are we going?"

He glanced over his shoulder and sped away—dirt and gravel kicking up to ping off the wheel wells. "Right now, I just need to get us far enough away from here, and then I can do the magic to banish this bad boy."

Twisting in her seat, she looked out the back window. "He doesn't seem to be following us."

Smoke billowed from the hotel, and blue-and-red flashing lights flickered across the building, the fading sound of sirens filling her ears. The hard pumping of her heart had thumped inside her ears with a deafening lub-dub a few minutes ago, so loud she hadn't even noticed the fire department's arrival. This night would definitely go down in history as her most exciting date. Ever.

"Don't count on it. Just because you can't see him doesn't mean he isn't following us."

She gave a mock laugh. "Isn't this where you're

supposed to lie and tell me everything is going to be okay?"

He smiled, revealing his sexy dimple again. "Everything *is* going to be okay. That's no lie. I won't let anything happen to you."

For some reason, she believed him. Wasn't sure why she did, but nonetheless she did. She looked around and noticed they were heading for the edge of the city. "Do you have a destination in mind?"

"A friend of mine keeps a travel trailer out this way for emergencies. I have all the ingredients I need to make the potion to banish the Helix Demon. I just need a few minutes to work on it. The trailer should be warded well enough to keep this particular demon at bay."

"Does the demon have a name?" She couldn't believe she'd actually just asked him this. Her head spun with all the information and her new understanding of what she considered reality.

He cast her a glance, his brow furrowed—as though trying to decide whether her question was sincere or making fun of him. "His name is Krulle." He faced the road again. "And he wants revenge for me sending his brother to the Zith realm."

"Hmm." She didn't know where to start—his answer spawned many new questions. "How many realms are there?" Seemed as good a place as any to start.

Jason laughed. "I can't believe you are taking this so well."

"Pfft." She laughed. "I don't know about well, but I'm trying to deal. And the nerd in me has to admit there is a level of coolness to all of this."

He grinned at her again, and she couldn't help the rush of desire swimming through her veins. She tried to shake it off. Having sex while being chased by a demon? Probably not a smart idea. And she really didn't want to think about the fact she indeed did want to have sex with Jason again. "How many realms?"

"Too many. I don't even know all of them. We tend to send the really bad ones to Zith. There, they can maim and kill each other. Also they can't escape. Well, honestly, I should say they can't escape easily. It would take the deaths of some pretty powerful witches and warlocks before they could."

He pulled off the main road and drove over dirt and rock. Nestled in a group of trees sat a travel trailer which had seen better days.

He reached into the backseat and removed a backpack. "We need to get inside quickly. Our friend will be here any minute."

No more incentive needed. Keeping all her limbs intact rode high on her to-do list. She jumped from the Jeep and dashed for the trailer. The camper could barely be called a rectangle, and, from the brief glimpse she got in the headlights, it had the wonderful brown-and-orange striping so popular in the seventies. She was skeptical about how it would provide protection for them against a mad, raging-bull dude, but if Jason thought so, then she didn't have much choice but to follow him.

He chanted something and the door opened, interior lights coming on. He motioned for her to precede him. She climbed up the rickety metal steps, bolted through the doorway, and gave the interior a quick scan, trying to decide where to move next. Her jaw dropped.

"Shut up!"

Laughing, he closed the door behind them and strode past her.

If she didn't know any better she'd have sworn she just walked into a five-star hotel suite equipped with a full kitchenette. Rich wines, greens, and tans decorated the inside. A few landscape paintings adorned the walls. Except one wall, where a huge flat screen TV hung. "This is awesome."

She turned and found Jason in the kitchen, pulling things from the backpack. *Right. Worry about demon banishing then look around the neat digs.* "Can I help with something?"

"You already are."

Susan ambled into the kitchen area. "How is looking around slack-jawed helping?"

"The fact you don't think I'm totally crazy is helping. Or the fact you aren't running and screaming."

She shrugged. "I'm a southern girl. We're made of pretty sturdy stuff."

Jason leaned over and captured her lips in a sweet, searing kiss. When his tongue sought entry to her mouth, she welcomed it. He tasted of their earlier lovemaking, mixed with danger and mysticism—a heady combination that had her moaning and leaning into him for more.

With a groan, he broke the contact, pulling her into his embrace. "When this is over," he murmured against her hair, "please give me the chance to make this up to you. No more secrets. I promise."

She tilted her head back. "First, you have to save me from the Minotaur guy. Then we'll talk." She winked at him, and he swatted her ass before turning his attention back to his potion making.

Susan leaned against the counter and watched him work. He had various herbs and dried things in jars. A few looked familiar. Others looked disgusting and smelled even worse when he took the lids off. Seeing him like this excited her on a whole new level. What would it be like to be a part of this world? And she thought he'd tried to hide the fact he was poor. She laughed.

"What do you find amusing?"

She blushed, not really wanting to admit the thoughts crossing her mind. But what the hell. They were done with secrets. "It's silly really."

"Tell me."

"I thought you were lying about your job because you were poor."

He lifted a brow. "Really? Well, I guess it's better than some things you could have thought."

The trailer rocked hard, a loud boom sounding outside. Susan grabbed the counter to keep from falling, and her heart sped up again. For a moment, she'd nearly forgotten about the raging-bull man who'd been following them.

Working in earnest, Jason added and heated ingredients in a small metal pot reminding her of a fondue-type setup. Another blast rocked them, and this time she stumbled and crumpled to the floor.

Oh my God! Will this tin can hold up against that raging maniac? She got to her feet. Jason strained the brew he'd made and emptied the contents into a glass vial. The liquid shimmered purple.

He clasped her upper arms, his expression all seriousness. "I need you to stay inside, no matter what happens, Susan."

"What! You're going out there?"

He cupped the side of her face and pulled her in for a quick, fierce kiss. "Don't worry. This is my job. I'll be back before you know it."

She gasped as he turned and headed for the door. "Be careful!"

He disappeared outside, the trailer door slamming shut behind him. She raced for the window, unable not to watch and afraid to all at the same time.

Jason crossed the small yard, his stride purposeful. His broad shoulders were back, and he looked formidable as any warrior of old. The bull hadn't made an appearance yet, but Jason scanned the area, alert and ready.

A fire ball hurtled toward Jason's head. Susan screamed. Jason feinted left, dodging the flaming sphere. It whirled past him and slammed into the side of the trailer. Blue flame erupted against the window, casting off immense heat. She toppled backward off the sofa. Scrambling to her feet, she realized the wall had held. She resumed her seat.

Outside, Jason went toe to toe with the hulking bull. He wrestled with the huge beast, white light coming from his palms. And damn if he wasn't winning.

Palms against the glass and face pressed in tight, she watched the battle in awe. Jason caught a hoof in the chest. It ripped across his red shirt, leaving it in tatters. Shrubs on the ground near the trailer blazed, and in the dim light she saw blood seeping from his wound.

But Jason recovered quickly and delivered a power-filled blow of white light against Krulle's face. The beast roared in fury and tried to sling another ball of fire. He dove to the ground, and it missed. Mesquite bushes ignited, crackling and popping. When the bull darted in Jason's direction this time, he rolled, more white light enveloping Krulle.

The bull ended up tethered in some type of ethereal light, and Jason made quick work around him. He grabbed a stick and drew a pentagram in the dirt, Krulle at its center. The beast snarled and roared with displeasure, fighting the restraints of illumination binding it to the ground.

Jason pulled the vial from his pants pocket. Walking in a circle around his hostage, he sprinkled the liquid over its large, grotesque body. His lips were moving, but Susan could hear none of his words over the racket the beast made.

Blue flames consumed the writhing monster, and it began to wail and scream, the sound unholy. Susan shivered. The wind picked up and swirled. A low vibration began in the walls and moved to engulf the entire trailer. Susan held on tight but didn't look away from the scene outside.

A bright-red glow started beneath Krulle and grew wider. Then he was gone. Vanished.

Everything went still, and Susan couldn't stop staring at Jason in amazement. He lifted his head and looked at her, concern lining his brow.

She ran for the door. When she swung it open, he climbed the metal steps and took her in his arms. He walked farther into the living room and kicked the door shut behind him.

"I'm so sorry you had to see that."

She pushed back against his shoulders. "Are you kidding? That was...it was...." She didn't know how to word it.

"Dangerous," he supplied.

She smiled. "Exciting!"

He shook his head in wonder. "How did I get lucky enough to find you?"

Susan wrapped her arms around his neck. "I don't know. I can't even express what I'm feeling right now. I've been through a range of emotions tonight for sure, but in the end, I can't say I'd change a thing."

He kissed her deeply, and she responded with enthusiasm. His erection prodded her lower belly, and she pressed more firmly against him. The adrenaline rushing through her system turned quickly into a fire of desire burning wildly.

Before she lost herself in the lust he created in her, she pushed away. "We need to look at your injuries."

He tried to pull her back, but she evaded him.

"I'm fine, Susan. The only thing paining me is not having you beneath me, writhing and voicing your pleasure."

A shiver of desire ran down her spine. Mere words from his lips turned her into a simmering sexual ball of unfulfilled passion. It was hard to push her need for this man aside, but concern for his well-being seemed to be the push she needed. "Then let me look at your chest."

He followed her into the kitchen. It took her only a few seconds to find a first-aid kit. She pushed at the remains of his shirt, wanting to free it from his gorgeous body so she could tend his wounds. Surprisingly, they weren't bad. She cleaned the blood away and put some ointment on them.

He watched her every movement, passion shining in his eyes. She closed the first-aid kit, and he took her hand in his, placing it on his bare shoulder. Without thought, she caressed him. His hands moved to her body. She sighed, loving the feel of his hands roaming her curves. Things heated quickly. His mouth descended on hers, and her hands went to the fastenings of his pants. He divested her of her dress with equal vigor.

Jason broke away from her mouth and kissed a trail down her neck. "Are you sure about this?"

"Yes. I want you." Everything was crazy and exhilarating. She wanted the mysterious man in front of her and all the drama that came with him.

He freed her breasts and palmed them in his strong hands. "You're so beautiful. I could make love to you all night."

A smile tipped the corners of her mouth. "Sounds like a good idea to me."

Leaning in, she nipped at the skin between his shoulder and neck then trailed kisses lower. He released her breasts and threaded his hands through her hair. Moving even lower, she came to rest on her knees before him.

"You don't have to do that." His words were husky and passion laced.

She cast him a wicked grin. "But I want to. Don't you want me to?" She freed his erection.

In a throaty whisper he replied, "God yes."

She licked the crown of his cock and loved his answering moan. His fingers tightened their hold on her locks, but the pressure wasn't painful. In fact, it turned her on even more. She traced her tongue along his shaft, teasing him. His muscles tensed, and she knew she drove him crazy.

Wetness coated her labia. She dipped her head forward and drew his dick into her mouth. Never had performing oral sex on a guy aroused her this much. She was attuned to each movement and breath he took, and adjusted what she did to maximize his pleasure.

She sucked him deeper into her throat. His cock swelled even bigger the more she took him in and out of her mouth. Precum coated her tongue, and she moaned, her desire for him climbing.

A growl filled her ears, and he pulled himself free of her lips. She didn't get much chance to react before he fell to his knees in front of her and turned her away from him. A quick jerk brought her back flush with his chest. He nipped at her neck and earlobe.

"You make me crazy with wanting you." He fisted her panties and tugged. The material bit into her flesh for a second then tore free from her body. "I hope those weren't your favorite," he growled near her ear. "You have me so turned on I need to be inside of you. Now."

His erection rubbed against her ass, and she bent forward, coming down on all fours. His hands splayed across her bottom. Then he trailed one lower, running his finger through her wet sex. She bit into her bottom lip, raw need filling her. Her pussy pulsed with anticipation.

"Wet and ready for me," he whispered.

She heard him tearing open a package behind her. The head of his cock traced her opening and then pushed inside. She sucked in a sharp breath, delicious sensations coursing through her cunt. His fingers bit into the flesh of her hips, and she bucked against him, wanting him to move inside her.

He gripped her harder to stay her movements. "I'm trying to get control. I don't want to hurt you."

"You won't. I want it rough." She wiggled her hips as much as she could. "Please."

With a curse, he pulled out and slammed back into her. She cried, pleasure spiking in her core. "Yes!"

He pistoned his hips roughly against her ass. The sound of his pelvis slapping her skin filled her ears. Their sounds of pleasure joined the mix. Her climax came quick, and she screamed, her pussy pulsing around his shaft. With a roar, he joined her in bliss, his dick spasming inside her.

Breaths rushing, they both collapsed to the floor.

He rolled to the side and brought her with him, spooning her.

"I shouldn't have been so rough with you. But with my adrenalin up and then you sucking me like that...I lost it."

She giggled. "I loved it. Don't apologize. And now that I know how to make you crazy horny, I can do it next time."

He kissed her neck. "You want a next time?"

"Definitely."

Epilogue

Susan yelped as the concoction in front of her fizzed and popped, splashing green yuck all over her safety goggles. Jason laughed, crossing the kitchen with a dish towel in hand.

"It's not funny. It's the third time I've screwed up this potion."

He pulled the goggles from her face and cleaned the other splatters from her skin, his mischievous smirk firmly in place. "I told you to go easy with the sage."

"I did."

Lifting the rag he'd used, he showed her the color of the mess on it.

"Okay, so I thought I did." She sighed and leaned

against the counter. "I'm not very good at this witch thing." She'd been working hard to learn from Jason for the past six months. She'd even left her job in New Mexico to move in with him once she found a secretarial position in Lubbock.

"You're doing fine. Brewing potions isn't easy. You'll get better with practice." He pulled her into his embrace.

"Yeah. You say that now, but what happens when I blow the house up?"

He shrugged. "We'll get a new one." His hands moved to her ass. "Just don't hurt this lovely body of yours in the process."

The taste of his lips would never get old. She sighed, opening her mouth to his seeking tongue and taking pleasure in the kiss he offered.

He ended the kiss with a nip of her bottom lip. "I have a surprise for you."

She smiled and wiggled her hips against his, teasing his erection. "I can tell."

He laughed. "No. Well. That, too, but I have another surprise for you."

"What?"

"I bought tickets today for San Diego."

She shook her head, confused. "What is in San Diego?"

He grinned, revealing the dimple she loved.

"Comic-Con."

Her heart rate accelerated. "Really!"

"Yeah. I thought it would be a good trip to take for our honeymoon."

She trembled, tears making her vision swim.

"That is if you'll say yes." He went down on one knee in front of her and clasped her hands in his. "Susan Kinlow, you have made me the happiest man in the world since I've met you. I would be honored beyond all measure if you would become my wife."

Wetness tracked down her cheeks, and she nodded fiercely. "Yes! Oh, yes! I would love to marry you." She fell to her knees and sought his lips with her own, their kiss laced with salt from her tears of happiness. "I love you so much, Jason."

"I love you, too. With all of my heart."

About the Author

Virginia Cavanaugh is a multi-published author of
erotic romance. Her work covers many sub-genres as
new characters present themselves to her every day.
After working for years as a nurse in pediatrics, her
love of the alpha hero sparked her desire to bring her
own stories to life. When not playing housewife,
mother, maid, laundress, taxi driver or just general
all-around slave, she enjoys finding a quiet corner to
read or work on her next story.

Also by Virginia Cavanaugh

Worth Fighting For
Tempting Her Tiger

www.ingramcontent.com/pod-product-compliance
Lightning Source LLC
Chambersburg PA
CBHW060955120626
46557CB00003B/1171